Seahorse Stars

Seahorse Stars

The Lost Lagoon

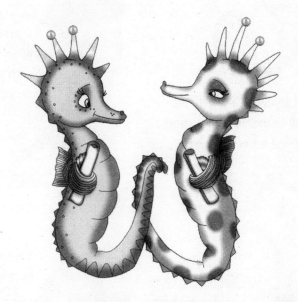

Zuzu Singer

Illustrated by Helen Turner

USBORNE

Meet the Pearlies

Fun and friendly CAMMIE is
a vivid pink seahorse who dreams
of becoming a Seahorse Star.

Shy but
sweet
CORA is
a pretty
pink seahorse
with pale
pink stripes.

Bossyboots
CORINETTA is
a golden seahorse
with a snooty
upturned nose.

Cammie's
best friend
JESS is
a born
storyteller.
She is a bright
bluey-green.

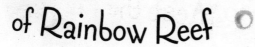

# of Rainbow Reef

Pale-green
MISS SWISH
is firm but fair
as the elegant
leader of
the Pearlies.

Brainbox BREE
knows all the answers!
She is purple with lovely
lavender fins.

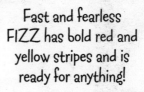

Fast and fearless
FIZZ has bold red and
yellow stripes and is
ready for anything!

Rainbow Reef

Coral Tower

Seahorse City

Eelgrass forest

Palace

Sandy Cove

Pearlie Pavilion

Cammie's House

Pink Sand Plains

Coral Caves

Seahorse Stars is dedicated to every child who
loves to read...including you!

First published in the UK in 2011 by Usborne Publishing Ltd., Usborne
House, 83-85 Saffron Hill, London EC1N 8RT, England.
www.usborne.com

Text copyright © Lee Weatherly, 2011

Illustration copyright © Usborne Publishing Ltd., 2011

A CIP catalogue record for this book is available from the British Library.

JF AMJJASOND/11 02341/1

ISBN 9781409520269 Printed in Reading, Berkshire, UK.

Chapter One

Cammie Sunbeam sighed happily as she and her best friend Jess swam through the warm waters of Rainbow Reef. Up ahead was the Pearlie Pavilion. It was almost time for their next Pearlie meeting, and Cammie could hardly wait!

"I wonder what our next pearl will be?" mused Jess. She was a pretty, blue-green

seahorse with sparkling eyes. Cammie was a bright, cheerful pink. Both girls wore two shiny pearls on their crowns, which they'd earned for their camping and first-aid skills.

"I don't know, but I can hardly wait to find out!" said Cammie eagerly. "Just think — only four more pearls to go, and then we'll be..."

"*Seahorse Stars!*" they exclaimed together. Twirling their tails, they spun about in the water.

Cammie giggled, feeling dizzy. The Seahorse Stars was the waviest club in Rainbow Reef. They got to go on exciting adventures, and do things to help the Reef. She'd wanted to be one for as long as she could remember!

But being a Pearlie is pretty great too, thought Cammie. She and Jess swam through the pink coral doors of the Pearlie Pavilion. Inside there were cosy areas for all the different Pearlie groups. Dozens of other young seahorses were there too, of every colour of the rainbow.

Cammie and Jess were both in the Dancing

Waves group. They swam over to their section, where some of the other girls were already waiting. There was Bree, a clever, purple seahorse; Fizz, who had red and yellow stripes and was very sporty; and Cora, a pale pink seahorse with long eyelashes.

Cammie was relieved to see that Corinetta wasn't there. Maybe the golden seahorse wasn't coming this time — it would be wonderful to have a meeting without her snooty comments for once!

"I hope we find out about our next pearl today," said Bree.

"Well, *I* just hope it's something exciting," said Fizz. "Like deep-sea exploring...or how about shark hunting?" Her eyes gleamed. "Yeah! Wouldn't that be wavy?"

"*Sharks?*" squeaked Cora, turning an even paler pink than usual. "Oh, no! I'm sure Miss Swish wouldn't let us—"

The others burst out laughing. "I think Fizz was kidding," said Jess gently.

"Oh," said Cora, looking embarrassed.

Cammie smiled. Though Cora tried really hard to do well, she was scared of everything! Even so, Cammie liked her. Only the week before, Cora had stood up to Corinetta when she had refused to help the others.

Just as Cammie thought this, Corinetta came swimming up, with her nose lifted grandly in the water. "Hello, everyone," she said. Then she saw Cora, and scowled. "Oh, it's *you*," she said, narrowing her eyes.

"Hi, Corinetta," mumbled Cora.

"Corinetta, aren't you feeling well?" asked Jess innocently. "You look really strange. You know, I think there's something going around…"

"Yeah, tail rot!" sniggered Fizz. "Your tail turns rotten and falls right off. The first symptom is that your face goes like this." She imitated Corinetta's glare. "You've got it, all right!"

"I feel fine!" snapped Corinetta as the others giggled.

"Well, I'm glad to hear it," laughed a tall, pale-green seahorse, swimming up behind her. It was Miss Swish, the Dancing Waves leader. She smiled warmly at them. "Hello, girls!"

Cammie smiled back with the others. She liked Miss Swish a lot. She was very fair and understanding, and knew everything there was to know about becoming a Seahorse Star.

Miss Swish glided to the front of their area. "Are you all ready to learn about your next pearl?" she asked.

Cammie's fins tingled with excitement. Finally, they were about to find out!

"Yes, Miss Swish," they all chorused, as they sat down on their shells.

Miss Swish turned to a piece of slate that sat on a coral stand. Taking a piece of chalk in her tail, she wrote *WAVE WANDERER* in big letters. Cammie stared at the words curiously. What did they mean?

"Can anyone tell us what the Wave Wanderer pearl is for?" asked Miss Swish.

Bree waved her fin in the water. Cammie wasn't surprised. The clever purple seahorse always knew the right answer...but she was so nice that everyone liked her anyway.

"The Wave Wanderer pearl is for finding our way around Rainbow Reef," said Bree. "And we'll get to use a map and a compass, just like the Seahorse Stars do!"

"That's right." Miss Swish nodded. "Very good, Bree!"

Jess raised her fin. "What's a compass?" she asked.

"It's a tool that tells you which direction you're going in," explained Miss Swish. "To earn your Wave Wanderer pearl, you'll use both a map and a compass to go somewhere you've never been before, and then find your way back again."

Cammie gulped. She wasn't very good at reading maps, or at finding her way around places. In fact, her family was always teasing her about how easily she got lost! *This pearl sounds really hard,* she thought worriedly.

"Wow, I can hardly wait to get started!"

exclaimed Fizz, bouncing up and down on her
tail. The others looked just as excited. Cammie
quickly put on a smile, so that no one would
know she was nervous.

The only seahorse who didn't seem happy
was Cora. "Um, Miss Swish...it isn't dangerous,
is it?" she asked.

"Oh, you're such a baby," muttered Corinetta.

Cora bit her lip, looking hurt. Cammie forgot her own worry as her fins went hot with anger. Corinetta was always saying things that made others feel bad. Cammie thought she'd give anything for the golden seahorse to be in one of the other groups!

Fortunately, Miss Swish had overheard. "Remember the Pearlie Rule, Corinetta," she said sharply. "You should always think of others before yourself...and that means *not* making fun of other seahorses!"

Corinetta gave Cora a sickly-sweet smile. "Sorry," she said.

Cammie and Jess rolled their eyes at each

other. They both knew that Corinetta wasn't sorry at all.

Miss Swish went on. "To answer your question, Cora, no, it's not dangerous. You'll only go places that are very safe to practise your Wave Wanderer skills."

Cora sighed in relief. Cammie felt a bit relieved, too. This pearl was going to be hard enough, without worrying about it being dangerous! She rubbed her fins together nervously.

What if the other girls laughed at her, once they saw how awful she was at finding her way around? And even worse...what if she didn't get her pearl?

Chapter Two

"We'll learn about maps first," said Miss Swish. "Now then, you all know that a map is like a small picture of a place, don't you?"

Cammie nodded with the others. She *did* know that...it just never helped when she was trying to figure out how to read them! She listened carefully as Miss Swish explained that

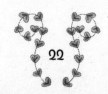

the top of a map always points north.

"Maps also have little drawings called *symbols* on them," went on Miss Swish. "And there's a place on the map that tells you what all the symbols mean. Does anyone know what it's called?"

Bree raised her fin again. "It's called the key," she said. "It's usually down at the bottom."

"That's right," said Miss Swish. "So if you saw a drawing like this on a map —" she drew a blobby-looking circle — "then you'd look at the key to find out what it meant." She smiled at them. "If we were making our own map, what do you think this might be?"

"It could be a place that has jellyfish!" giggled Jess.

"Good!" Miss Swish wrote *KEY* in big letters. Then, drawing the blobby circle underneath it, she wrote *JELLYFISH*. "So you'd know to be very careful if you were swimming through an area that had *that* symbol on it," she said.

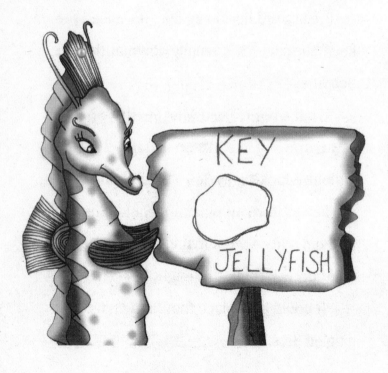

"Yes, or else the jellyfish might get you…
zap!" cried Fizz cheerfully, tickling Cora.

Cora squealed as if there really *were* jellyfish
nearby. "Maybe…maybe we should make it
something else, that's not so dangerous," she
said timidly.

Corinetta rolled her eyes and snorted.
Cammie glanced at her. She knew that if Miss
Swish hadn't been listening, the golden
seahorse would have said something mean
again!

"Jellyfish will do fine, Cora," said Miss
Swish. "Now then, maps also have something
called a *scale*. Who knows—" Bree waved her
fin in the water. Miss Swish sighed. "*Besides*
Bree," she said.

Cammie's heart pounded. She hoped that

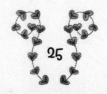

Miss Swish wouldn't call on her — she had no idea! Then Cora hesitantly raised her fin. "Does it mean...how far away things are from each other?" she asked.

"Yes, that's right," said Miss Swish. She held up a map of Rainbow Reef. "For instance, this isn't *really* the size of Rainbow Reef, is it?"

Everyone giggled. "No, the real thing is a bit bigger," said Jess with a grin.

"Of course it is!" said Miss Swish. She propped the map in front of the board. "Say that we want to go from *here* to *here.*" She pointed at two places on the map. "That's only about a fin long on the map, but we know it's much further than that really. So how would we find out how far we were going?"

"It says at the bottom—" burst out Bree,

and then she stopped short. "Sorry," she said sheepishly.

"That's all right," said Miss Swish with a chuckle. "But you're right, Bree. We'd just look at the bottom, where it says *scale*. Then we'd find out that every one of these little boxes on the map is really one wave long. So to find out how far we're going, all we have to do is count the boxes."

Cammie gazed at the map. Everything Miss Swish had said made sense, but she still felt worried. She knew that when she tried to use a map herself, it would be very different!

I bet I'll be the only one who can't make head or fin out of it, she thought glumly.

Miss Swish put the map of Rainbow Reef away. "Let's draw a map of Seahorse City," she

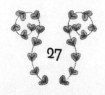

suggested. "Here, I'll start us off." She drew the Pearlie Pavilion on the board. Everyone laughed when they saw that she'd added a tiny seahorse with pearls on her crown!

Miss Swish smiled. "Would someone like to add the library to our map? Fizz?"

The striped seahorse swam to the front. Cammie was very glad that Miss Swish hadn't called on her. She could find the library in real life, but wasn't at all sure where it would go on the map!

But Fizz didn't hesitate as she took the chalk and started to draw. "I think it's right about... here!" she said.

Fizz's library looked a bit wobbly, thought Cammie. But she must have put it in the right place, because Miss Swish nodded. "Good!

Now, how about the town hall? Jess?"

One by one, she called the seahorses up to add to the map. To Cammie's dismay, none of them had any problem putting things in the right place. Her crown felt hot with embarrassment. *Please don't call on me!* she thought as hard as she could. *Please don't call on me, please don't...*

"We only have the Guards' Coral Tower left to add," said Miss Swish finally. "Cammie, would you like to do that?" She held out the piece of chalk.

Cammie swam slowly forward. Where was the tower from here? She had no idea! She just knew that it was near the palace.

Suddenly Cammie realized that she didn't *have* to know exactly where the tower was.

All she had to do was put it near to the palace,
which Corinetta had already drawn. Quickly
finding the palace on the map, Cammie drew
the tower just above it.

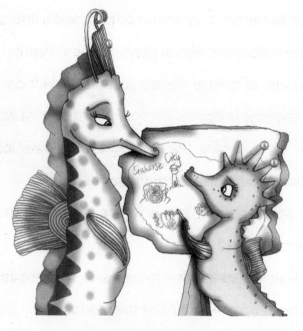

"Very good!" said Miss Swish with a smile.

Cammie breathed out in relief. She'd got

it right!

"Now, I'd like you each to draw a map of all your favourite places," said Miss Swish. She passed out blank sheets of eelgrass and coloured chalk. "For instance, you might have your home on it, and your school, and a special place where you like to play...and the Pearlie Pavilion, of course!" Her eyes sparkled kindly.

Cammie drew her home. She spent a lot of time on it, hoping that their time would run out before she had to add anything else. What if she put something in the wrong place, and the others laughed at her?

Bree raised her fin. "Miss Swish, is there any more pink chalk? Mine's almost gone."

Miss Swish looked in the coral supply cupboard. "I'll just go over to the White Sands group, and see if we can borrow some," she said. "Keep drawing, everyone!"

The moment Miss Swish was gone, Corinetta let out a bored sigh. "This is *so* easy," she said. "Honestly, who doesn't know how to do this baby stuff?"

Cammie felt her face turn warm.

"Well, I think it's interesting," said Jess. "I've learned loads today."

Corinetta made a face. Then she looked across at Cora, and her eyes narrowed meanly. Obviously, thought Cammie, she was still cross about Cora standing up to her the week before, and getting her into trouble with Miss Swish!

"Let's see your map," she said, grabbing Cora's map away from her.

"Hey!" Cora tried to get it back, but

Corinetta swam upwards, holding it out of her reach.

"Are these all your favourite places?" she taunted. "Home...school...boring...boring..." She stopped suddenly. "Hang on, don't you live near the Crystal Caves? How come they aren't on your map?" She smirked. "I know! It's because they're too *scary* for you, isn't it?"

"It is not!" cried Cora, still grabbing for her map. "I hadn't finished yet!"

All at once Cammie had had enough of Corinetta. Swimming up out of her seat, she snatched the map away from Corinetta and handed it back to Cora.

"Thanks," mumbled Cora.

Corinetta looked taken aback for a moment. Then she tossed her head. "Ooh, the little scaredy-crab has someone to protect her," she sneered.

Cora's eyes filled with tears. Anger sizzled through Cammie. Without thinking, she burst out: "Well, she wasn't scared of you last week, when she stood up to you! And you deserved it, Corinetta. You're mean and horrible — everyone thinks so! I wish you weren't even *in* the Pearlies!"

Chapter Three

There was a stunned silence. Then a few of the Dancing Waves sniggered, and Cammie gasped as she realized what she had said. Corinetta's face turned red as she glared at Cammie. Cora, on the other fin, was gazing at Cammie as if she were a hero!

Just then Miss Swish returned with the pink

chalk. She looked at the three girls in surprise. "What's going on?" she asked.

Cammie swallowed hard, wondering what she could say. To her surprise, Corinetta spoke up. "Nothing, Miss Swish," she said. "We were just looking at Cora's map."

Miss Swish didn't look convinced. She shook her head. "Well, sit down now and finish your own maps."

Cammie swam back to her seat, her cheeks blazing. "Cammie, that was great!" whispered Jess in her ear. "You should have seen her face!"

Cammie winced. She *had* seen Corinetta's face...and it had made her very nervous!

More than that, she could tell that she had hurt Corinetta's feelings. Cammie was glad that she'd stopped Corinetta from picking on Cora, but she knew she shouldn't have said the things she did — and in front of all the other Dancing Waves, too! No wonder Corinetta was furious.

Soon it was time for Pearlies to be over. Miss Swish handed out maps of Rainbow Reef for

them all to take home. "These are yours to keep, so that you can start practising with them," she said. "Try finding your house on them, and then see if your parents will help you to explore a bit!"

Cammie took her map with a heavy heart. She knew without looking at it that she wouldn't be able to read it. Everyone was going to laugh at her when they realized how bad she was!

But right now she had other things to think about. As everyone started to leave, Cammie hurried to catch up with Corinetta. "Corinetta, listen," she said, swimming in front of her. "I'm really sorry about what I said..."

Corinetta's eyes flashed. "Believe me, you *will* be sorry," she hissed. "You just wait,

Cammie — I'll get you for this!" Turning suddenly, she sped off through the water. Cammie stared after her in dismay.

Jess swam up beside Cammie. "Wow, did you see how cross she looked? I've never seen her *that* angry before."

"Me neither," said Cammie weakly. What a great day this had turned out to be! Not only was she worried about getting her pearl... but now she'd made a real enemy out of Corinetta.

"Did you have fun at Pearlies today?" asked Cammie's mother at dinner that night. Like Cammie, she was a vibrant pink. Cammie was very proud of her mother, who was one of the guards who kept Rainbow Reef safe.

Cammie tried to smile. "Yes, it was great," she said.

"What's your next pearl going to be?" demanded Tigg, Cammie's little sister. Tigg was very excited that Cammie was in the Pearlies. She could hardly wait until she was old enough to join, too.

Cammie cleared her throat. "Um...the Wave Wanderer pearl," she said.

Cammie's father appeared from the kitchen. He was holding a shell full of sweet seaweed for dessert. "Isn't that the one where you have to read maps?" he asked.

Cammie nodded glumly. "Yes, and use a compass," she said. "To earn our pearl, Miss Swish says we have to go somewhere we've never been before, and then find our way back again."

Stripe, Tigg's twin brother, sniggered. "Oh, you'll be great at that," he teased. "You get lost just swimming out the door!"

"Hush," said Cammie's mother, tapping him on the head. "Cammie, would you like me to help you practise?" she asked.

Cammie brightened a bit. "Would you?" she asked. She knew how busy her mother was.

"Of course!" said her mum warmly. "We'll have a practice session right after dinner."

"Us too, us too!" cried Tigg, bouncing up and down in her seat.

"No, not you," snapped Cammie. That was all she needed – her little brother and sister hanging about, laughing at her!

"We'll play something else until it's time for you two to go to bed," Dad promised the twins. "We need to leave Cammie alone." He winked at Cammie, and she smiled back at him. Her dad was great. He always understood!

But even with Mum's help, Cammie could hardly work out where she was on the map. It was all so confusing! She turned the map upside down and sideways, trying to make sense of it.

"Look, we're *here*," said Mum again, pointing. "Now, can you find the Coral Caves?"

Cammie and her siblings often played hide and seek in the Coral Caves. Even so, she frowned as she stared at the map. She knew where the Coral Caves were in real life...finding them on the map was something else again!

"Um..." Cammie turned the map around.

"Are they here?" she asked finally, pointing with her fin.

Mum shook her head. "No, that's the Pinkfins' house," she said gently. Cammie winced. The Pinkfins' house was nowhere near the Coral Caves!

"Here, let's go to the caves now, and you can follow the way on the map," said Mum. As they swam through the warm water, Cammie clutched the map tightly, trying to work out where they were going.

"You're holding it upside down," pointed out Mum, turning the map over in Cammie's fins. Cammie felt her cheeks turn hot. Oh, great!

When they got to the Coral Caves, Mum said brightly, "Now, how about somewhere else? Can you take me to Sandy Cove from here?"

But it was the same again. No matter how hard Cammie tried, she couldn't find Sandy Cove on the map. She ended up taking them to the Eelgrass Forest instead!

Mum had to show her the right way to Sandy Cove, and even then Cammie knew that she didn't have the hang of it.

Finally it started to get dark. "Come on, we'd better call it a night," said Mum, steering her back to their house. "Don't worry, sweetie, you'll get it...just keep practising!"

Cammie's tail sagged glumly as she got ready for bed. She hoped her mum was right... but deep down, she wasn't sure at all. Map reading was just as hard as she'd thought it would be.

How was she ever going to earn her pearl?

Chapter Four

When it was time for their next Pearlies
meeting, Cammie found herself swimming more
slowly than usual. Jess stopped in the water,
waiting for her to catch up. "What's up?" she
asked. "You're creeping along like an old crab!"

Cammie lifted a shoulder. "I don't know...
I suppose I'm not looking forward to

seeing Corinetta again."

Jess grinned. "You mean after you told her off so brilliantly?"

"Yes, that," groaned Cammie. "Jess, she was furious! And you know how mean she can be."

Her best friend shrugged. "So? She deserved it, she really did. Besides, she won't do anything with the rest of us there!"

Even so, Cammie felt nervous as the pink walls of the Pearlie Pavilion came into view. She wasn't the sort of seahorse who got into arguments very often. She didn't like rows — they made her stomach go tight and funny.

"Cammie, wait!" called a voice.

Cammie looked up in surprise as Corinetta came speeding up. "I've been wanting to talk

to you all week," panted the golden seahorse, bobbing in the water.

Cammie blinked. "You...have?" she faltered.

Corinetta nodded hard. "Yes, I wanted to tell you how sorry I am for how I acted last time." She bit her lip. "You were right, Cammie. I — I was really mean to Cora. I'm going to apologize to her, too."

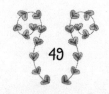

Cammie's mouth dropped open. She glanced at Jess, who looked just as shocked as she was. Was this really *Corinetta*?

"Well — that's nice of you," said Cammie.

"I'm glad you think so," said Corinetta, opening her eyes wide. "Because I've been thinking about what you said. Does everyone *really* think I'm rude and horrible?"

"Uh…" Cammie didn't know what to say.

"Yes," said Jess bluntly. "Though sometimes you're just rude. Or just horrible."

"I'm not talking to *you*," snapped Corinetta. Then she seemed to catch herself. "I mean… thanks, Jess. I'm going to try really hard to be nicer from now on."

Jess blinked in surprise. Corinetta smiled at them both. "Well, see you inside!" she said brightly, and swam off into the Pavilion.

Cammie stared after her. This *couldn't* be for real…could it? She and Jess followed Corinetta into the Pavilion. Jess shook her head, looking baffled. "That wasn't like Corinetta at all! I wonder if she's feeling well?"

As the two girls arrived at the Dancing Waves section, Corinetta was talking to Cora. "I'm *really* sorry for how I acted last week, Cora," she said earnestly. "I didn't mean all those awful things I said."

Cora looked as astounded as Cammie had felt. "Oh…that's all right," she said, staring at Corinetta. The other Dancing Waves were gaping at her, too.

Cammie sat down in a daze. She and Jess exchanged a glance. Corinetta, *apologizing*?

It didn't seem possible!

Miss Swish arrived just then, carrying a coral box. Corinetta sat down on the other side of Cammie. "I hope we learn more about map reading today," she whispered in a friendly voice. "It's really wavy, isn't it?"

Cammie had been so amazed by Corinetta that she'd almost forgotten her trouble with maps. Now it all came back to her. "Yeah, really wavy," she said, holding back a sigh.

"Hello, everyone!" said Miss Swish cheerfully. She put the box down. "Have you all been practising with your maps?"

"Yes, Miss Swish," said everyone.

"It was *so* much fun!" added Fizz. "My parents and I went on a picnic to the Pink Sand Plains. I led us the whole way there and back!"

"Me too!" said Bree, swishing her tail excitedly. "We went to the Eelgrass Forest. Following my map was really easy, once I got the hang of it."

The other Dancing Waves chimed in with similar stories. Cammie squirmed in her seashell chair. It didn't sound like any of the others had got lost, or held their map upside down! She wished that she could just vanish away into the sand.

"How about you, Cammie?" asked Miss Swish.

Cammie nodded quickly. She *couldn't* admit that she was the only one who wasn't able to read her map. "Yes, it was great! We went all around my house, and — and to the Coral Caves, and the Sandy Cove — and to the Eelgrass Forest, too!"

It wasn't really a lie, she told herself uneasily. They *had* gone to those places...she just hadn't found them on her map!

"That sounds like fun," said Miss Swish with a smile. "Well, since you're all doing so well with your maps, I think we should talk about compasses!"

She took the lid off the coral box. Cammie sat up straight, trying to look as interested as the others. Inside, she felt cold with dread. What if compasses were as hard as maps?

"Here's a compass for each of you," said Miss Swish, passing them out.

Cammie stared at hers. It was a pair of curved shells that came together like a clam. When she opened the top shell, she found a round piece of glass with letters on it. A long, black pointer wobbled as she turned the compass this way and that.

"Now then, compasses do something very special," said Miss Swish. "They always tell us which way north is. Look down at your compasses. Do you see the pointer? It's pointing north!"

Jess raised her fin. "But mine says it's pointing south," she said, sounding confused. "At least, I think it is. Is that what the *S* stands for?"

Miss Swish nodded. "That's right. You have to turn your compass until the letter *N* is lined up with the pointer. *N* stands for north. Everyone do that now!"

Concentrating hard, Cammie slowly turned her compass. Miss Swish swam around to check everyone's.

"Good!" she said, swishing her pale-green tail. "Remember, no matter where you are, your compass will always point north. All you have to do is line up the *N* with the pointer. So that means you can use them to help you with your maps, too!"

Bree raised her fin. "Miss Swish, how does the compass work?"

"With magnets," explained Miss Swish. "You see, the biggest magnet in the world is the North Pole, and your compass always wants to point towards it."

Cammie gazed at her compass in awe. It was hard to believe that something as far

away as the North Pole was affecting it!

Bree's forehead wrinkled in thought. "But then…what happens if you get near another magnet?" she asked.

"Then your compass would try to point towards it instead," said Miss Swish. "So you should always be careful to stay away from them."

Corinetta glanced at Cammie with her eyes narrowed, as if she were thinking something. Then she saw Cammie looking and gave her a big smile. Cammie blinked. *What* was Corinetta up to?

But she didn't have time to worry about it. Suddenly Miss Swish turned to Cammie and said, "Now, Cammie, which way is west?"

Cammie was startled. How should she

know? They'd been talking about *north*, not *west*! She stared down at her compass. If her pointer was pointing north, then that *W* on the dial must stand for west. And that meant…

Hesitantly, Cammie pointed towards the door of the Pearlie Pavilion. "Is it…that way?" she faltered.

"Exactly!" beamed Miss Swish. "Well done, Cammie. Does everyone understand?" She looked around at them all, and smiled. "Excellent! Then let's go out and have a practice."

"That was *so* great, Cammie," said Corinetta as the Dancing Waves swam out of the Pearlie Pavilion together. She gave Cammie a friendly nudge. "I bet you're really good at this. You figured that out in no time!"

"Er…thanks," muttered Cammie.

Jess giggled. "It looks like you've got a new fan," she whispered in Cammie's ear.

Cammie made a face. She still wasn't sure what Corinetta was up to…but for the moment, she didn't care. She smiled down at her compass. Perhaps she wasn't going to be hopeless at using it after all!

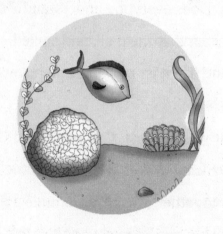

Chapter Five

To Cammie's delight, using a compass was easy. She and the other Dancing Waves had great fun practising, calling out directions to each other. The only annoying thing was Corinetta. The golden seahorse seemed determined to stick by Cammie's side, smiling and being friendly. She was everywhere Cammie turned!

I almost liked her better when she was nasty, thought Cammie in exasperation.

Finally it was time for Pearlies to be over. "Keep practising," Miss Swish told them. "Next time we meet, we'll do a practice run for earning your pearl...and then the time after that will be for real."

Cammie gulped. In all the fun of learning to use a compass, she'd forgotten her troubles with map reading. Now they came rushing back to her. *I'd better work really hard,* she thought nervously. *Or else I won't have a chance!*

For the next few days, Cammie did just that. But map reading still made her head spin. Even if she figured out where *she* was on the map, working out where she should go after that seemed impossible!

"What are you doing?" asked Stripe, swishing up to Cammie as she stared at her map outside their house.

"Practising," said Cammie shortly. Her mum had promised to go out with her again later that day, but for now she was practising on her own. She wasn't doing very well at it, either!

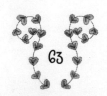

Stripe peered over her shoulder as Tigg came swimming up, too. "Oh, that's easy," he said cheerfully. He pointed at the map with his fin. "Look, we're right there, and—"

"Ooh, yes," said Tigg, bouncing in the water. "And the palace is *there* on the map, and—"

Argh! Cammie quickly rolled her map shut. "I'm going to go and practise somewhere else," she said tetchily. "*Alone.*" And before her brother and sister could say anything, she had swum off with the map under her fin.

Even with her mum's help, Cammie knew she hadn't improved much by the time the next Pearlies meeting came around. She felt very nervous as she and Jess swam to the Pearlie Pavilion. They were having their practice run today! Why hadn't she told Miss Swish about the problems she was having? It felt too late now to put her fin up and confess that she didn't have a clue.

Maybe it'll come to me, somehow, fretted Cammie.

"Are you okay?" asked Jess.

Cammie nodded, swishing to one side to avoid a school of silvery fish. "I'm worried about map reading, that's all," she sighed.

Jess looked sympathetic. "It hasn't got any easier?"

Cammie shook her head. "No, and now it's almost time for—" She broke off as Corinetta came zipping up.

"Cammie, Jess, hi!" she said breathlessly, bobbing up and down in the water. "I'm *so* glad to see you. Can I swim to Pearlies with you?"

Cammie almost groaned out loud. That was all she needed! "I suppose," she said grumpily.

Corinetta didn't seem to notice Cammie's mood. She chattered cheerfully as the three of them swam towards the Pearlie Pavilion. "I can hardly wait for our practice run today," she said eagerly. "It sounds like *so* much fun!"

"Mm," said Cammie.

"Yes, you like trying for your pearls, don't you, Corinetta?" said Jess innocently. "They look *so* good on your beautiful crown." She tossed her head, imitating Corinetta.

Cammie held back a snigger. Corinetta was very proud of her unusually tall crown, and was always boasting about it!

For a moment the golden seahorse's eyes seemed to narrow. Then Cammie thought she must have just imagined it, because Corinetta gave a friendly grin. "Ha, ha – that's really funny, Jess!" she laughed. "I suppose I *do* brag about my crown too much, don't I?"

Cammie blew out a breath. "*What* is going on with you, Corinetta?" she demanded. They swam into the Pavilion with the other seahorses.

Corinetta blinked. "I don't know what you mean."

"You do, too," insisted Cammie. "You're just being so...so..." She waved her fins about.

"*Nice*," finished Jess for her. "It's making us nervous, Corinetta. If you're up to something, could you please just do it and get it over with?"

To Cammie's surprise, Corinetta looked really hurt. "I'm not up to anything," she protested. "I told you last week...I'm sorry for how I've been acting, that's all. But if I've been bothering you, then...then I'll leave you alone." She swam slowly away.

Cammie and Jess looked at each other. "I don't believe it," said Jess, shaking her head. But she didn't sound very sure of herself.

Neither was Cammie. As she and Jess took their seats in the Dancing Waves area, she peeked across at Corinetta. The golden seahorse was sitting on her own, gazing sadly at the sandy floor.

Cammie bit her lip. Was it possible that Corinetta truly *was* trying to be nice? Maybe she was so out of practice that it sounded strange, when she really meant it.

Miss Swish arrived then. "Is everyone ready for your practice run today?" she asked cheerfully.

Cammie gulped. She couldn't waste time thinking about Corinetta now — she had more than enough to worry about!

Miss Swish seemed to notice how nervous she was. She gave Cammie a friendly smile. "Now, I don't want anyone worrying about this," she said. "It's just for practice — and it's meant to be fun!"

Cammie tried to smile.

Miss Swish explained to everyone how the

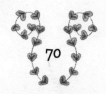

practice run would work. "The goal is to bring back a pebble like this one," she said, holding up a bright blue pebble. "I've hidden six of them in different places around the Reef, one pebble for each Dancing Wave. To find yours, you'll have to follow directions using both a map and your compass."

Oh, why couldn't it be just our compasses? thought Cammie fretfully. She'd do really well then!

Cora raised her fin. "Can we work in pairs?" she asked.

Cammie looked up hopefully. If she and Jess could go together, she'd be fine! But Miss Swish shook her head. "No, I'd like you to do this on your own," she said. "It'll be better practice for when you try for your pearl for real."

She pointed to a coral box on the table. "First, each of you will take a map from this box. The maps all follow different routes, but will take you to the same thing: a pufferfish, who's waiting for you! He'll give each of you compass directions. Just follow those, and find your pebble. Then come back here as fast as you can!"

All around Cammie, the girls were smiling at the thought of the pufferfish. Cammie thought wistfully that it *did* sound like fun… if only she knew how to read maps! Slowly, she swam forward to collect a map from the box like the others.

"All right, you've got half an hour!" announced Miss Swish. "Ready…steady…GO!"

Everyone raced out of the Pearlie Pavilion, where they stopped and unrolled their maps. Cammie gulped. Her map looked really hard, with drawings of eelgrass and coral and sandy ocean floors all over it. There was a drawing of a pufferfish, too, and a dotted line showing how to get to him.

Cammie frowned. She could see the Pearlie Pavilion on the map, but which direction was she supposed to go in? It wasn't clear at all!

Jess hovered nearby, looking worried. "Are you going to be okay, Cammie?" The other girls had all sped off already.

Cammie nodded, and tried to smile. "Yes, I'll be fine! You go on, Jess. I think I've just about got it worked out."

"Well…if you're sure…" said Jess finally. "Good luck!"

Once her friend had gone, Cammie stared at the map again, turning it upside down and sideways. She didn't have it almost worked out at all, of course! She had no idea which way to go. Hurriedly, she chose a direction and swam off. Maybe this would be the right way.

The dotted line on the map went past a large rock. Cammie swam and swam, staring worriedly around her. No rock came into view. Wait — was *that* a rock, over there in the distance? She zoomed over to it. But it was just a sleeping sea turtle. He blinked grumpily as Cammie came speeding up.

"You woke me up!" he grumbled. "You young seahorses have no respect." He glided off through the water, muttering to himself.

What *now*? Cammie bit her lip and looked down at her map again. None of it made any sense. She had no idea how to get to the pufferfish. And if she couldn't do that, then she couldn't find her blue pebble to bring back.

Cammie felt tears prick at her eyes. She was going to be the only Dancing Wave to fail the practice run!

Chapter Six

Now everyone will know how hopeless I am, thought Cammie miserably. *There's no way that I'll get my pearl when the time comes for real!*

"Cammie, what's wrong?" said a voice.

Cammie stiffened as Corinetta came swimming up. "Nothing," she said quickly.

"Look, I've just got my pebble," said

Corinetta, holding up a small blue stone. "I'm on my way back now."

"Good for you!" snapped Cammie.

Corinetta blinked. "Um...do you need some help?" she asked.

Cammie started to say no, and then she stopped. What good was pretending? She *did* need help...even if Corinetta wasn't the seahorse she'd have chosen to ask. She took a deep breath.

"Sort of," she muttered. "I'm lost. I — I can't work out my map."

Something like a sneer crossed Corinetta's face. It was gone so fast that Cammie thought she must have imagined it.

"Why not?" asked Corinetta, sounding concerned.

"I don't know," confessed Cammie glumly. "I've never been able to work out maps. It takes me ages to find where I am on them, and then I can't work out which direction I should go in."

"But you've got your compass," said Corinetta.

Cammie blinked. "So?"

Corinetta made a sound like a snort. Then she smiled, and Cammie thought it must have been a cough instead.

"Don't you remember?" she said. "North is always *up* on a map. So since you have your compass, you can find which way north is. Then just line your map up with that, and you'll know what direction you should go in."

Cammie gasped as she suddenly

remembered Miss Swish saying the same thing. She had been so worried that she'd forgotten all about it! Quickly taking out her map, she did as Corinetta had said. To her amazement, the map suddenly became much clearer. She could even find where she was on it!

"Then the pufferfish must be...*that* way," she worked out, turning to point behind her. "I went in the exact wrong direction!" Excitement fizzed through Cammie. "Corinetta, thank you!" she burst out. "You really helped me."

Then she stopped, blinking in confusion. "Um...why did you?" she asked.

Corinetta widened her eyes. "Cammie, I've been telling you and telling you! I want to make up for how I acted before, that's all. I'd like to be your friend now." She smiled at Cammie again.

Cammie smiled uncertainly back. Corinetta *had* seemed really hurt earlier. Maybe she had misjudged her. "Okay," said Cammie, making up her mind. "Friends!" She offered the tip of her tail to Corinetta, who shook it with her own.

"I'd better go and find the pufferfish now, so I can get my pebble," said Cammie. "But Corinetta...thanks again!"

Corinetta grinned at her. "Oh, anything for a friend," she said sweetly.

Now that Cammie could read her map, she found the pufferfish easily. He grinned at her as she came speeding up. "Another seahorse!" he said cheerfully. "Would you like your compass directions?"

"Yes, please!" cried Cammie.

Looking important, the pufferfish blew in a breath, so that he turned as round as a bubble.

"*Swim twenty-two tail-lengths north, then go fifteen north-east,*" he recited, bobbing in the water.

"Thanks!" Quickly, Cammie took out her compass again, checking it for north. A moment later she was zooming off, counting tail-lengths as she went. Twenty-two north... now fifteen north-east...she should be there!

Looking up, Cammie saw that she'd reached a tall, thin piece of coral. Checking all around it, she found a bright blue pebble tucked into one of its holes. Hurrah, she'd found it!

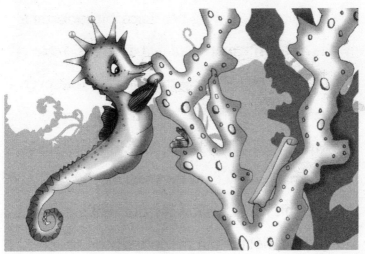

Clutching the pebble tightly, Cammie swam back to the Pearlie Pavilion, and made it with time to spare. Smiling widely, she showed her pebble to Miss Swish. "Well done!" exclaimed the Dancing Waves leader. "Did you have any trouble with the practice run?"

Cammie hesitated, glancing at the others. Most of them were back by now, and were sitting in their seats, talking. "Well…a little bit," she admitted, lowering her voice. "It took me a while to get the map reading part right. You see, I — I've been having trouble with that ever since we started."

Miss Swish raised her eyebrows. "You were? But Cammie, why didn't you tell me?"

"I don't know," said Cammie, looking down. "I — I just felt stupid. I've always been really bad at map reading, so I knew right from the start that I wouldn't do well."

Miss Swish shook her head. "You should always go into things with an open mind, Cammie," she said gently. "It's hard to do well at something if you keep telling yourself that you're going to fail!"

Cammie blinked in surprise. Could Miss Swish be right? *Had* she made things harder for herself?

"But then you found your pebble after all," said Miss Swish. "How did you do it?"

"Corinetta helped me," said Cammie. She explained what the golden seahorse had told her. The other Dancing Waves were all listening now. They stared at Corinetta in surprise.

Miss Swish looked pleased as Cammie

finished. "That's exactly right! Well done, Cammie — and well done you, too, Corinetta," she added. "I'm glad to see you helping someone out."

Cammie expected Corinetta to preen at the praise. Instead Corinetta looked almost shy. "That's okay," she said modestly, fluttering her fins. "I was just really happy to help."

"I'm still not convinced," whispered Jess as Cammie sat down next to her. "Corinetta being nice is like…like the tide going sideways! It just doesn't happen."

"But look at how she helped me," pointed out Cammie. She smiled, remembering how great it had felt to find her pebble. "I don't know, Jess…I think maybe she really means it after all."

A few days later, it was time to try for their pearl for real. Cammie sat with the others, her heart pounding. She'd been practising hard ever since their last meeting. Though she could hardly believe it, maps really made sense to her now. She knew she had a real chance of getting her pearl – thanks to Corinetta!

"Can I see your compass?" whispered Corinetta as they waited for Miss Swish to get started.

Cammie was startled. "Don't you have yours?"

The golden seahorse nodded. "Yes, but I think something might be wrong with it. I just want to compare it to yours, that's all."

Cammie hesitated for a moment, but then told herself she was being silly — she and Corinetta were friends now. After all, if it hadn't been for Corinetta, she still wouldn't know how to read maps!

She handed her compass over. "There you go," she said.

"Thanks." Turning away slightly, Corinetta bent over both compasses for a moment. "No,

I guess I was wrong," she said finally. She
handed the compass back to Cammie. "Thanks
for letting me check, though."

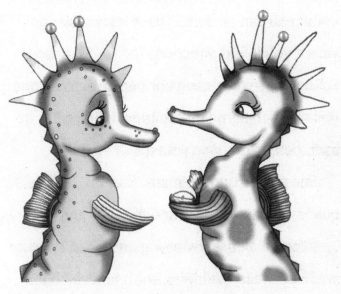

"That's okay," said Cammie. The two
seahorses smiled at each other.

"Is everyone ready?" asked Miss Swish.

"Yes, Miss Swish," said the Dancing Waves
together. Cammie shivered with excitement.

She could hardly wait to get started!

"All right, here are your maps," said Miss Swish. "They're a bit trickier this time, but I know you can all do it! The *X* marks the spot where you'll find directions for your compass. Follow those to get to your pebble — a red one this time! To earn your pearl, you'll need to be back here in an hour with it."

She passed out the maps. Cammie and Jess quickly squeezed tails for luck.

"You've all been working hard, and I'm sure you'll do well," said Miss Swish kindly. "But if you run into any trouble, don't panic — just stop and check your map and your compass! Good luck, everyone! Ready...steady...GO!"

Chapter Seven

The Dancing Waves shot out of the Pearlie Pavilion. Once outside, Cammie hurriedly opened her map. There was the *X*, in the middle of a small lagoon a few waves away.

Opening up her compass, Cammie turned it to face north...and then paused. Surely north had been to the *left* of the Pavilion last time?

But now north was straight ahead.

Cammie shrugged. *I must be remembering it wrong,* she decided. North was north — it couldn't move about! Looking at her map, Cammie sped off towards the lagoon.

After a while, the pink coral below her changed to sand...and then to green coral... and then back to sand again. But where was the lagoon? She should have got there by now!

Cammie stopped and checked her map. Her forehead creased in confusion. This didn't make any sense! She was *sure* that she'd got it right.

Maybe I'd better go back to the Pearlie Pavilion and start over, thought Cammie nervously. Turning on her tail, she swam back as fast as she could. Soon she was outside the walls of the Pearlie Pavilion again. None of the

other seahorses were in sight. Of course not —
they were all off getting their pebbles!

Cammie turned her compass to the north
again. No, she hadn't been mistaken...north
was straight ahead. But *where* was the lagoon
in that case?

Cammie hurried back the same way she'd
gone before, peering about her worriedly. Had
she missed it, somehow? But how did you miss
a lagoon? *I bet I didn't go far enough,* thought
Cammie. *I just need to keep going, and I'll get
there!*

She swam and swam. After a while, her tail
and fins started to feel tired. Surely the lagoon
couldn't be *this* far away? It felt like she'd been
gone ages. Soon an hour would have passed,
and she wouldn't have found her pebble.

Cammie's eyes felt hot with tears. And here she'd thought that she'd been doing so well! It looked as if she wasn't going to get her pearl after all. *I knew it,* she thought miserably, wiping her eyes. *I'm just not any good at direction!*

A passing clownfish looked worried when he saw her. "What's wrong, little seahorse?" he asked. "Can I cheer you up?" Turning a flip in the water, he waggled his fins at her, making a funny face.

"Thanks," said Cammie, trying to smile. Clownfish hated to see anyone unhappy!

"That's better!" said the clownfish with a grin. He sped off.

Somehow Cammie felt a bit better after that. She looked down at her map again. She really didn't see how she had gone wrong… but somehow she had. *I've got to figure it out quickly,* she thought. *I'm running out of time!*

Miss Swish's words came back to her: *If you run into trouble, don't panic…just stop and check your map and your compass!* Cammie frowned in confusion. But she *had* checked her map and her compass, and she was still going in the wrong direction!

Could her compass be broken? Cammie gazed down at it. Suddenly she remembered how Corinetta had borrowed it — the way that she'd turned away from Cammie, not letting her see what she was doing.

Cammie gasped as a thought hit her like a tidal wave. Had Corinetta done something to her compass? *No way,* she told herself, horrified. *Corinetta's my friend!* Was she, though? Uneasily, Cammie remembered the slight sneer that she'd seen on Corinetta's face, when the golden seahorse had taught her how to read maps.

Biting her lip, Cammie looked her compass over carefully, turning it this way and that. Her eyes widened. There, just under the circle of glass. There was a slight mark, as if someone had lifted it up!

Cammie raised up the glass...and, hidden

under the compass rim, she found a small grey
stone. Taking it out, she stared at it in
confusion. Then she noticed that the pointer
on her compass had moved. Slowly, Cammie
waved the stone around the compass. The
pointer spun, following the stone wherever
it went.

A chill ran down Cammie's spine. "*A magnet!*" she whispered. Corinetta had wedged a magnet into her compass, so that the pointer would point towards it instead of north!

Furious, Cammie shoved the magnet into the pouch at her side. How could she have been so *stupid*? Corinetta had only pretended to be her friend, so that she could get back at Cammie for telling her off. Even when she'd helped her learn to read maps, it had only been to gain Cammie's trust, so that she could trick her into handing over her compass!

Cammie pushed her angry thoughts away. She didn't have time to worry about it now. She had to go and get her pebble — as fast as she could!

* * *

Racing back to the Pavilion, Cammie started over again. This time her compass showed that north was to the left, just as she'd remembered. Swimming faster than she'd ever swum before, Cammie sped to the lagoon. She found it easily this time — a tropical paradise with blue, sparkling water.
And there was the shell with her compass directions on it, leaning against a piece of coral!

37 tail-lengths → E
14 tail-lengths
↓ S

Grabbing it up, Cammie sped off again. Thirty-seven tail-lengths east...fourteen south... Using her compass, she raced through the water, leaving a trail of bubbles behind her.

Finally she came to a small hole in a wall of bright yellow coral. There was her red pebble, just where it was supposed to be! Hurriedly, Cammie tucked it into her pouch and started back to the Pearlie Pavilion.

Oh, her tail and fins ached! But she had to keep swimming, as fast as she could. *I'm not going to make it,* thought Cammie tearfully. The thought made her swim more slowly. What was the point? She'd already failed, she knew it.

Then Cammie remembered something else Miss Swish had told her: *It's hard to do well at something if you tell yourself you're going to fail.*

Cammie's snout rose up determinedly. She might still have a chance — and as long as there *was* a chance, then she was going to do her best! Fluttering her fins so fast that they could hardly be seen, Cammie shot through the water.

"Hey, watch where you're going!" squawked a parrotfish.

"Sorry!" called Cammie over her shoulder.

Finally, the Pearlie Pavilion came into view. Cammie sped even faster than before. She tore through the pink coral doors and raced over to the Dancing Waves section.

The other girls were all back already. Each of them had a shiny new pearl on her crown. Corinetta scowled, not looking at all pleased to see her.

"Cammie, you made it!" cried Jess, jumping up and down in the water.

"Oh, well done!" exclaimed Miss Swish. "And with half a minute to go! Did you get your pebble?"

Half a minute! If she'd given up, she wouldn't have made it. Cammie nodded, gasping. "Yes — I've got it..." She reached into her pouch. She could feel both the magnet and the pebble. All at once an idea came to Cammie.

She took out the magnet. "Oh, I wonder where *this* came from?" she said. Holding it up, she looked pointedly at Corinetta. The golden

seahorse looked ill suddenly, as if she'd swallowed a sand flea!

Hiding her grin, Cammie put the magnet away and brought out the red pebble. "Here you are, Miss Swish. I'm sorry I took so long to get it...I, er, took a wrong turn."

Miss Swish smiled. "Don't worry, you found your pebble and got back in time, and that's what counts! I'm very pleased to give you your Wave Wanderer pearl, Cammie. You've earned it!"

Standing up straight, Cammie beamed as Miss Swish placed a third pearl on her crown. She'd done it, she'd really done it!

"Hurrah!" shouted Jess, spinning on her tail. Everyone crowded round Cammie, congratulating her...except for Corinetta.

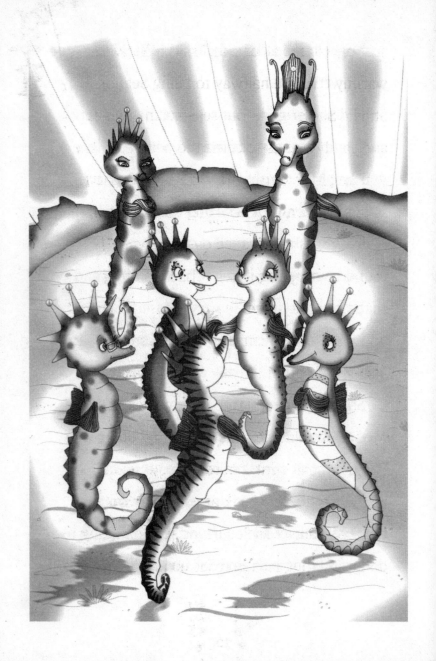

"Well done, all of you," said Miss Swish warmly. "You're halfway to being Seahorse Stars!" She brought out seaweed munchies and sandy sweets to celebrate with.

The girls chatted and giggled as they ate, swapping stories of how they'd found their pebbles. Corinetta sidled over to Cammie.

"Are you going to tell Miss Swish?" she asked in a low voice.

Cammie glared at her. "I *should*," she said coldly. "That was a really mean trick, Corinetta."

Corinetta made a face, scowling down at the sand. "All right, I'm sorry," she said. "I — I just wanted to get back at you for telling me off, that's all. I wasn't sure what I was going to do at first, but then Bree asked about magnets, and that gave me the idea..." She trailed off, and then said hurriedly, "You won't tell Miss Swish, will you?"

Cammie glared at her. *How* could she have ever believed that Corinetta was really her friend?

"*Are* you going to tell Miss Swish?" asked Corinetta, fluttering her fins nervously. "I promise I won't do anything like that again, not ever."

Part of Cammie did want to tell Miss Swish. But she knew if she did, Corinetta would get into terrible trouble. She might even be thrown out of the Pearlies! And as awful as Corinetta had been, Cammie couldn't quite do that to her. After all, Corinetta had taught her how to read maps — even if it had only been part of a trick!

"I *might* not tell," she said slowly. "But only if you promise to be nice to Cora from now on."

Corinetta nodded hard. "I promise! I'll be *really* nice to her, not just pretending."

"All right, I won't tell Miss Swish," said Cammie finally.

Corinetta's fins sagged in relief. "Oh, *thank you*!" she burst out. "Honestly, Cammie — you won't regret it!"

She swam off. A moment later, Cammie heard her talking to a startled Cora. "You know, I've been thinking that the two of us should be friends," said Corinetta, linking her tail through Cora's. "We're both the prettiest, and we both have *really* tall crowns…"

Cammie rolled her eyes. Some things never changed!

"What was that all about?" asked Jess, swimming over to join her.

Cammie explained in a whisper. Jess's eyes widened. "No way!" she exclaimed. "I *knew* she was up to something. Of all the sneaky tricks!"

"But don't tell anyone else, Jess," added Cammie quickly. "I got my pearl anyway, and that's what matters."

Jess nodded thoughtfully. "Yes, and who knows? Maybe she really *will* be a bit nicer now." She nudged Cammie with her fin. "In fact, this could be the best thing that's ever happened to us! Now come on, there are still a few of those sandy sweets left."

As Cammie talked and laughed with her friends, she gazed proudly up at her third pearl. Despite everything, she had done it! She'd proved to herself that she really *could* read maps...and now she was halfway to being a Seahorse Star.

I wonder what our next pearl will be? thought Cammie eagerly.

She didn't know...but she could hardly wait to find out!

The End

Dive in with Cammie and her friends and
collect every splash-tastic tale in

Seahorse Stars!

The First Pearl   ISBN 9781409520245

Cammie is thrilled to be a member of the Pearlies
— the waviest club in Rainbow Reef. Her first task
is to go camping. Will she keep her cool, or
is she in too deep?

First-Aid Friends   ISBN 9781409520252

When Cammie's best friend shows a natural talent for
first-aid, Cammie gets competitive...and soon it's their
friendship that needs patching up!

The Lost Lagoon   ISBN 9781409520269

Cammie is confused by compasses and lost when
it comes to maps, so earning her Wave Wanderer pearl
is proving tricky. When stuck-up Corinetta
offers to help, Cammie is grateful. But can
Corinetta be trusted?

Danger in the Deep ISBN 9781409520276

Cammie loves studying for her Sea Safety pearl
and learning about the dangers of the Deep. So when
her little sister disappears, it's up to Cammie
to rescue her...

Coming soon...

Dancing Waves ISBN 9781409520306

All the seahorses must work together if they are
to earn their Tidal Team pearl...and they've chosen
Cammie as their team leader. Can she stop them
squabbling and help them come out on top?

The Rainbow Queen ISBN 9781409520313

To get her last Proficiency Pearl, Cammie must do
a good deed in Rainbow Reef...and then she will be a
Seahorse Star! But when Cammie begins her task, she
realizes the Reef is in danger, and she must ask
the Queen for help.

For more wonderfully wavy reads
check out
www.fiction.usborne.com